THE
Shark Island
Mystery

M. A. Harvey

Design & Illustration: Garry Walton

Chrysalis Children's Books

First published in the UK in 2004 by
Chrysalis Children's Books
An imprint of Chrysalis Books Group plc
The Chrysalis Building
Bramley Road, London W10 6SP

This edition is distributed in the U.S. by Publishers Group West

Illustration by Garry Walton 2004
Text © M.A. Harvey 2004

The right of M.A. Harvey to be identified
as the author of this work has been asserted.

ISBN 1 84458 147 0

British Library Cataloguing in Publication Data
for this book is available from the British Library.

Printed in Great Britain by Creative Print & Design (Wales) Ltd
10 9 8 7 6 5 4 3 2 1

CONTENTS

A message from

XTREME ADVENTURE INC

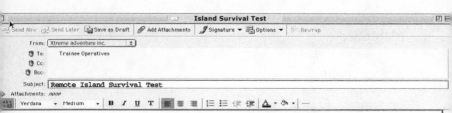

Send Now · Send Later · Save as Draft · Add Attachments · Signature ▼ · Options ▼ · Rewrap

From: Xtreme adventure inc.

To: Trainee Operatives
Cc:
Bcc:

Subject: Remote Island Survival Test

Attachments: *none*

Verdana ▾ Medium ▾ **B** *I* <u>U</u> T

XTREME ADVENTURE INC.
confirms that you are authorized to read this top-secret
transmission.

To: Trainee operative.
Re: Indonesian island survival training test.

XTREME ADVENTURE INC. is an organization dedicated to
protecting the planet and those who inhabit it. Our operatives
are an elite squad who have proved their bravery, survival skills,
and brainpower. They can survive in the most dangerous, hostile
places on Earth, and we call on them for rescue missions so
tough that all others would fail.

Do you have what it takes to join us? We shall see.

This training manual contains an adventure story. Imagine that
you are kidnapped and marooned on a mysterious island. All that
and more happened to Theo Kitt and Chris Brown. This is their
story. We will call it...

THE SHARK ISLAND MYSTERY

WILL YOU MAKE
THE GRADE?

In each chapter of this story there are quizzes
for you to complete. They will test your
brainpower and observational skills.

As you read through, keep a record of your
answers to the puzzles and quizzes.

Then check your credit score at the back of
this book to see if you have what it takes to join
XTREME ADVENTURE INC.

Finally, turn to page 125 to try for a place in
our ELITE SQUAD.

WARNING

Trainees who look at the answers before finishing the story will fail automatically as this shows lack of discipline and inability to follow instructions. These are serious flaws for XTREME ADVENTURE operatives.

Good luck to all trainees.
Chief of Field Operations

Marooned

The sky was unbelievably blue, lined along the horizon with a strip of silver cloud. The sea was an equally impossible-looking travel-brochure blue that glittered in the sun as a handsome white yacht pushed across it, threading its way through a maze of islands off the coast of Indonesia.

For a 14-year-old boy called Chris, the picture was so completely different from home, he could have been on another planet. He was leaning over the guardrail at the very front of the boat, hoping to be the first passenger to spot a dolphin. He thought he was alone until, turning, he glimpsed another boy, about the same age, sitting in a corner out of everyone else's view.

Chris caught the boy's eye.

"I can't believe I'm here, can you? It's wicked, isn't it! I've been pretending that I'm really, really rich and this is my very own yacht," Chris grinned.

The boy gave a weak smile, as if he was embarrassed. Chris decided the boy was probably shy.

"I see you're a Bobcats' fan," the boy remarked, glancing at Chris's jersey. Chris took this as a signal to be friends, and he walked over and sat next to the boy. Seeing them together, both in baseball caps, a stranger might have thought they were brothers, though they'd actually never met before. Chris was freckled, and his brown hair was cropped short under his cap. That's how all the boys wore their hair in the city where he lived. He was wearing his Bobcats jersey, baggy shorts, and the new sneakers his grandma had bought him for the trip. They'd been too expensive for his mom to afford.

The other boy also had brown hair, but it was longer, and curls escaped from under his cap. He was wearing a plain t-shirt, but also had baggy surfer shorts and a pair of cool sneakers. Chris was surprised that he hadn't seen him before in their group of tourists, when everyone had met up earlier at the dockside.

The boy had stowed a travel bag firmly under his knees, as if he didn't want to be parted from it. This helped give the impression that he was nervous.

"So, you're a contest winner, too," Chris said cheerfully. "The other people who won are all inside. I brought my mom. Who did you bring?"

The boy seemed not to hear, or was too shy to reply, so Chris continued.

"I was totally amazed when I won a vacation! Bet you were, too, huh? Me! Chris Brown, winning a trip to a millionaire's luxury vacation resort! Awesome!"

"You mean Koh's Landing?" the other boy replied.

"Yeah. That's where we're all going, isn't it?

It's owned by some multimillionaire man, the one who bought the Bobcats. I can't remember his name."

"Errol Kitt," the boy replied.

"That's right, Errol Kitt," Chris imitated an upper-class accent. "When my friends heard that I'd won, they said Errol Kitt was trying to make himself look good by giving away prizes to ordinary kids. I said they were just jealous. Yeah, he's probably horrible. Stinking rich people usually are, they say. But I'm not complaining. I got a vacation!"

The boy didn't reply, and there was an awkward silence before Chris thought of something else to say to him: "What's your name?"

"Theo," the boy replied.

"Right. Mine's Chris."

There was another silence, during which Chris tried to think of some way to make Theo open up a little.

"Stay here for a minute. I'll go in and find my mom. She's got some candy," he grinned and bounded away. When he got back he found

Theo studying a sheet of paper spread open on his knees.

"Here you are. Some chocolate to remind you of home," Chris handed Theo a candy bar.

"Thanks. Look, there's Koh's Landing," Theo smiled, pointing to the piece of paper. It was a map showing lots of different-sized islands, scattered like a handful of rice across the ocean.

"Weird name," Chris remarked.

"It's named after a famous local pirate, Koh, from about two hundred years ago," Theo explained, seeming to become interested in the conversation for the first time. "He was notorious. He had a whole fleet of pirate boats."

Theo seemed to know a lot about it. Maybe he had read up before he came.

"Well, I can't wait to get to Koh's place. It's going to be millionaire-living all the way. Easy huh?" Chris laughed.

Theo became quiet again, and Chris wondered what to talk about next.

"Do you like the Bobcats?" he asked eventually, but Theo had turned his head away.

"That's rude," thought Chris, but then he

followed Theo's gaze and saw that his attention had been caught by a motorboat that was powering quickly through the waves toward their yacht.

"We're slowing down," Chris remarked.

Over the boat engines, another, softer noise sounded behind them.

Click. Click.

As they swung around, their world turned into something new and terrifying. Two guns pointed at them, held by two men whose faces were set in hard, aggressive stares. Theo's eyes flicked up to see movement through the screen of the boat's bridge. He saw another gun, this time being held to the captain's head.

It looked like mutiny.

"W...w...what...what do you want?" Theo's voice stuttered, as if his words had been shaken apart by the sight of the long, black, gun barrels. The men didn't reply.

Chris recognized the guns from computer games he'd played. They were machine guns. The real thing.

Where was his mom? Was she going to come

out from inside the yacht? Was she OK? He didn't know what to do or what to say. His stomach felt as if it was dissolving from the inside out.

"You are being kidnapped," one of the gunmen said in a flat monotone. "Do not try to escape, and nobody else on the boat will be hurt."

He glanced from Theo to Chris, and a flicker of indecision crossed his face.

"Which one...?" he began, but was interrupted by a shout. The yacht had slowed to a stop and was wallowing in the waves. The motorboat had drawn up beside them and another gunman had climbed up a boarding ladder to the yacht deck.

"Into the boat!" he yelled, poking his gun into Chris's back.

"Mom!" Chris screamed. An arm pulled over his mouth to shut him up. He tried to bite it.

Theo was already being pushed over the side and manhandled into the waiting motorboat. Chris was almost thrown down behind him. The other gunmen jumped over the yacht's railing to join them. One tossed Theo's travel bag in. They pinioned the boys to the floor of the motorboat, and the pilot revved up the engine.

Chris was desperate to look up, to see his mom, but his head was being held down by one of the gunmen. The motorboat sped away, bumping over the waves.

Eventually the gunmen released Chris and Theo and left them to huddle on the floor, trying to turn their faces from the sea spray that whipped across their skin. The roaring noise of the engine, the thwap-thwap of the hull hitting the sea surface, the guns... It was as if they'd been forced through a screen into a violent action movie.

The boat roared past several islands and then turned toward a shape on the horizon. As it came closer, the boys could see that it was an island with a peak rising up from its center and a wide crescent-shaped bay fringed with a white sandy beach. Out in the sea a ring of white foam crashed around it and spat as the ocean hurled itself against a coral reef.

The motorboat slowed down and inexplicably approached the dangerous reef. The boys clung to the boat seats. They had no life jackets, and if the boat turned over they would be dashed onto the reef. Why was the pilot taking them so close to disaster? Chris flinched. Theo shut his eyes tightly.

Suddenly the boat shot forward. The pilot had aimed at a narrow gap in the reef, a safe channel that led them to the calm waters of a lagoon that lay between the reef and the shore. The lagoon water was shallow, and the boat quickly bumped the bottom. The pilot cut the engine.

"Get out," one of the gunmen ordered, motioning with his gun toward the beach. The boys did as they were told. There was no choice, but Theo grabbed his bag as they splashed into the water, and the gunmen let him take it. They waded ashore, and one of the kidnappers followed, carrying a plastic sack full of water bottles taken from the back of the boat. He dumped the sack on the beach.

"You stay here. There is no escape," he ordered. Then he waded back to the waiting boat, which powered back out to sea.

"They're going! Hey! You can't leave us here!"

Chris shouted, but the men ignored him. "They can't abandon us!" he cried.

Theo stood as still as a statue, with a mixture of sea spray and tears running down his face.

"I think I'm having a nightmare," Chris said, shaking his head in disbelief.

"No. This is really happening," Theo spat, and a look of bitterness settled on his features.

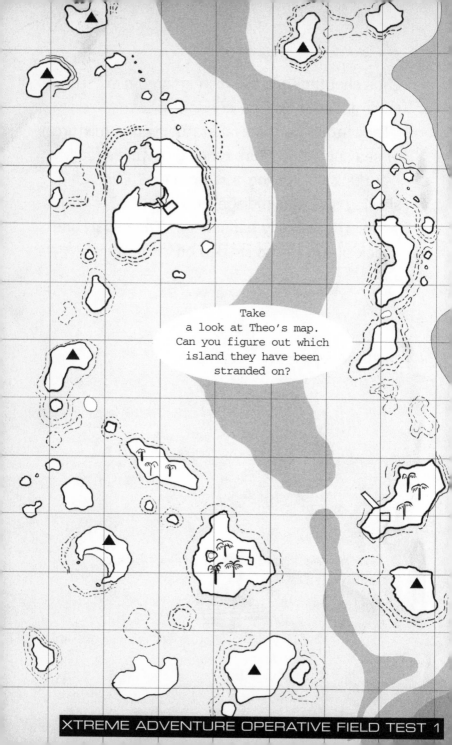

Knowledge of tropical islands would help you in a situation like this. Test how much you know. Keep a record of your answers and check them when you finish the story.

XTREME ADVENTURE QUIZ 1

1. What is a coral reef?
a) A bank of rocky material built by tiny creatures
b) A bank of mud and seaweed

2. What is a lagoon?
a) A stretch of wide beach
b) A stretch of shallow seawater

3. What landscape would you find in a tropical place?
a) Jungle
b) Desert

4. The water in a lagoon is:
a) Very calm
b) Very choppy

5. Waves crash up against a reef. Do they:
a) Crash against the outside edge?
b) Crash against the inside edge?

6. Indonesia has lots of islands. Where is it?
a) In South America
b) In Southeast Asia

A Bad Night

"So much for 'luxury island retreat,'" Chris muttered, kicking the sand angrily. "What a joke. What a dump. And what the hell happened to us?" he shouted.

Theo just stood there silently.

"Aren't you even angry?" Chris asked, glaring at him.

Theo's eyes blazed. "Angry? Yes, I'm angry," he replied in a voice full of seething resentment for something or someone.

"Why didn't that multimillionaire have some kind of security on board his stupid yacht?" Chris fumed.

"Shut up!" Theo was shouting now.

Chris snapped back, "What? You think this is OK, do you?"

"Shut up!" Theo screamed.

Chris was stunned. He stared at Theo.

"Look, I'm sorry. I shouldn't have shouted," Theo said, and seemed to crumple.

"OK," Chris said, dropping his voice. There was no point in arguing. After all, they were both in this crazy situation together.

"Why do you think they took us?" Chris pondered disbelievingly.

Theo changed the subject: "Help me lug these water bottles up the beach. I guess they're for you and me. The kidnappers don't seem to want us to die of thirst."

But Chris was still trying to make sense of what happened.

"Why snatch two ordinary boys?" he asked.

Theo glanced at him, seemed about to speak, then looked away.

"Let's get the water up the beach," he mumbled.

Between them they carried the plastic sack up the shore. It was edged by tropical trees and

shrubs that stretched up toward the hill above. There were no buildings.

They sat down on a rock to get their breath back and took a swig of water. The air was hot and damp, and seemed to be getting muggier by the minute.

"It's got to be some kind of joke. My mom's going to be livid that they didn't warn us about it," Chris said. "I wouldn't want to be in Errol Kitt's shoes when she gets hold of him. What do you think your parents will do?"

"See those clouds banking up? Rain's coming. Do you have any idea how to build a shelter?" Theo asked.

Chris was surprised and confused into silence by the way Theo seemed to ignore the things he said. The boy was weird.

"Well, do you?" Theo asked, more urgently.

"Uh, well, I went camping with the Cub Scouts once, and we made something out of branches. I suppose we could try that, and maybe use the plastic sack as a roof." Chris hesitated.

"Right, let's go," Theo snapped, and got up abruptly. He piled the water bottles in a shaded spot, then folded up the plastic sack and turned to leave the shore.

Chris shrugged. He'd come to a conclusion. There was no way this stupid situation was going to last long. Help was bound to arrive quickly. When they were rescued everything would be explained.

They walked further inland among the trees.

Suddenly Chris stopped and pointed. "Look, aren't those the ashes of an old fire? Someone's been here before." He glanced around and saw a few other signs that humans had once been in the area.

"Odd..." Chris thought. It was a mystery they couldn't solve now, though. They had to concentrate on getting shelter.

They found a stream running down the slope, clear of trees on either side.

"This will be ok for a site. See if you can find some big branches lying around. We'll have to make a frame," Chris explained.

They scouted around and gathered a few broken branches, barely enough to make a tent shape. They stuck the branches into the ground and tried to lash them together with strands of leaves pulled from nearby bushes.

"Ow, these leaves are really sharp!" Theo complained.

"Do you have something to help us cut them?" Chris asked, reaching for Theo's bag.

"No!" Theo snatched it away.

"Come on," Chris replied, and tried to grab the bag again.

"Get away from it!" Theo screamed. He picked up his bag and ran.

"Theo, don't be crazy! We have to work together. Don't be a quitter!" Chris cried furiously after the retreating figure.

Theo didn't reappear, so Chris finished the frame of branches as best he could and stretched the plastic sack over it. The light was fading, and the wind was growing stronger. It wasn't long before rain came, and it was soon clear that the shelter wasn't going to keep much of it out.

When the wind wrenched the plastic sack off the roof, Chris crawled out and was immediately hit in the face by the lashing rain. He also realized that his feet were sinking into soggy ground. The stream was flooding, and the site was turning into a swamp. The fast-disintegrating shelter was totally useless. He blundered into the darkness, back toward the shore.

The lagoon looked black and choppy now, illuminated every few minutes by lightning. He could hear angry crashing waves hurling themselves harder against the reef.

He struggled along the shoreline, soaked through. Sheets of rain seemed to be closing in on him, obliterating the rest of the world.

He felt desperate and ready to collapse to his knees in despair. He blinked through the raindrops to try to clear his vision and see where he was going.

That's when he saw a figure running toward him through the blur.

The boys didn't build their first shelter correctly, and it blew away in the storm. Would you do better? Try this quiz and check the answers when you have finished the story.

XTREME ADVENTURE QUIZ 2

1. Don't camp too close to a stream because:
a) It might flood
b) It might poison you

2. Should you dig a toilet:
a) Upwind of your shelter?
b) Downwind of your shelter?

3. Should you build your shelter:
a) On sloping ground?
b) On level ground?

4. Would you build your shelter with:

a) Branches that have been dried out and dead for a while?

b) Branches that have recently dropped from a tree?

5. To make a roof for your shelter, would you use:

a) Leaf-covered branches?

b) Mud?

6. Would you position the entrance to your shelter:

a) Facing away from the wind?

b) Facing the wind?

Nightmare Lagoon

"Chris! Chris! This way!"

A voice carried to Chris on the wind. A hand touched his shoulder. The running figure turned out to be Theo.

"Chris, I found a cave. Come on!" Theo urged, and led Chris around the curve of the lagoon, where a cliff began to rise up from the edge of the beach. A crack in the rock opened into a cave. It smelled of seaweed, but at least they were out of the rain.

Chris was shivering.

"Change into some dry clothes." Theo handed Chris a few things from his bag.

"OK. Thanks," Chris replied. They sat silent and

exhausted, huddled in the dark, as rain torrents, thunder, and lightning took over the night outside.

Chris started to develop an obsession about how hungry he felt.

"I wish I was back home with my mom, watching TV, and having a cheese sandwich," he said ruefully.

Theo nodded.

"That sounds nice. Tell me about where you live," he said.

Chris was grateful for the question. It took his mind off the cheese sandwich. He told Theo about his little house, his friends, and how they met in the park for skateboard contests, his mom, his dad, and his grandma, and his bedroom plastered with Bobcats' posters.

"How about you?" he asked Theo, but Theo didn't reply.

"You're . . . rich, right?" Chris ventured. "These clothes you've lent me . . .They're really expensive designer labels."

Theo sighed. "Yes, I'm from a rich family." He looked away. "I don't see them much. I go to boarding school," he added.

"Like Harry Potter?" Chris asked.

"Not really. There's not much magic around. It's OK, though," Theo replied, shrugging. "My parents got divorced ages ago. I don't see my mom all that much, or my dad."

"That's tough," Chris sympathized. He hoped Theo wasn't going to cry.

Theo didn't. He changed the subject in that weird way he had.

"I have some cereal bars," he said and delved into his bag. He brought out a box of bars and handed one over.

"Yes! Food!" Chris almost cheered with relief, and the subject of families was dropped as the boys munched their bars.

Neither of them dozed much, though they tried. They were awake when the morning dawned, bright and clear. The storm had passed and it looked like it was going to be very hot. In daylight they could see their cave clearly.

"If we were staying it would make a good base. We could clear the stones out and maybe line the floor with dry leaves," Chris suggested. "But

I'm sure we'll get rescued today. This is all some kind of mistake," he added.

"It's not a mistake," Theo said.

"What do you mean?" Chris replied.

Theo looked at him unhappily. Then he stomped away up the beach.

Chris shook his head. "Weird," he muttered. He started clearing the stones out of the cave, piling them up outside. He was certain they'd be rescued soon, but clearing the cave was something to do.

Meanwhile, Theo began to search the ground between the beach and the trees, building up a collection of driftwood and tree branches. He worked silently and angrily, then sat near the cave and tried to lash the branches together with sea grass.

Eventually, Chris sat down beside him. It was obvious that Theo wanted to make a raft, and there was absolutely no way it was going to work. Theo didn't admit that out loud, but he stopped struggling with it.

"Hey, how about some spearfishing?" Chris suggested, trying to be positive.

"Yeah. Yeah, OK," Theo agreed. He selected a long straight branch from his pile and broke off the end with his foot to make it jagged. He took off his sneakers and socks and waded into the shallow lagoon.

Chris thought about joining Theo but decided to let him splash around by himself for a few minutes. Theo was looking happier out there. That was good.

"The water's really warm," Theo cried.

"You'll scare the fish with all that splashing," Chris called. Theo nodded and waded back to shore.

"I've got an idea. I'm going to set a fish trap," Theo announced.

He found an empty plastic water bottle and unscrewed the top.

"I need bait," Theo said and dug around in his pocket, bringing out a piece of cereal bar. "I was saving this for dinner, but the fish might like it," he grinned, pushing it inside the bottle and holding it up for Chris to see.

"Fish will swim in through the neck of the bottle, and maybe they won't find their way out," he explained.

"I think that may be the nuttiest thing I've ever heard," Chris laughed. "But try it."

Theo paddled back into the lagoon and wedged his bottle under a rock. Then he returned and sat beside Chris on the beach.

"I was never in the Cub Scouts," Theo remarked as he shaded his eyes from the sun. "I've never done anything like camping. I have to stay...safe."

"Oh," Chris replied, not sure what to say. Theo's life didn't sound like much fun at all.

"Did you ever learn how to make a campfire?" Theo asked.

Chris couldn't remember much about Cub Scout camp, except that his socks got wet and they'd eaten loads of baked beans. But he could just about recall the firemaking.

"I think we found some moss and sticks, and we put those on the ground. And then we piled bigger pieces of wood on top..." he began.

"We could do that," Theo declared.

"Yeah, but then the Cubmaster lit the moss with a match. We don't have any matches,"

Chris smiled apologetically. "Look, why don't you go and check your fish trap? I'll think about this fire thing," he suggested.

Theo splashed into the water while Chris tried to figure out how they could light a fire without matches. He'd heard of people rubbing sticks together to get a spark, but that sounded as if it would take ages. What he needed was a lens or a mirror to focus the sunlight onto a pile of dry sticks. He'd seen that done on TV.

Theo's bag lay on the ground by the cave entrance. Chris looked toward Theo, now wading further out into the lagoon waters.

"I'll look for a mirror. It won't do any harm," Chris thought. He began to look through the contents of the bag. There were clothes, a book, some washing supplies . . . and then his fingers closed around a frame.

He lifted it out.

It was a photo of Theo, in a Bobcats' jersey, on the pitch at the Bobcats' stadium. He was standing between the star player and another man, and they were holding up a trophy the Bobcats had won.

"Wow! Lucky Theo!" Chris remarked. He himself had won the vacation to Koh's Landing, getting the ticket at a Bobcats' game. He assumed the same thing had happened to Theo, but with the extra bonus of holding up the trophy.

He ran his fingers over the glass in the frame. "I could use this glass to focus the sunlight, if Theo would let me take it out of the frame," he muttered to himself.

He went back down to the water's edge and called to Theo, who turned to him and waved. That's when Chris's eye caught something behind Theo's shoulder, farther out at the edge of the reef.

"Theo! Theo!" he screamed. "Get out of the water! There's a shark!"

Theo looked around and saw for himself the unmistakable shape of a shark's fin protruding from the surface of the water.

He began to run, splashing back to shore.

"Come on!" Chris screamed wildly.

The white-tipped fin pointed toward Theo. Underneath was a long, sleek, black shape.

It was cruising in, attracted by the splashing.

As Theo ran, his heart pumped hard with fear, and a throbbing filled his head.

The water seemed to hold him back. It was like wading through thick mud. His legs felt super-heavy.

"Don't stumble," Theo thought. He stepped on a sharp rock but ignored the stab of pain that shot through his foot.

He was getting closer to shore now, but where was the shark? He stole a glimpse behind him and wished he hadn't when he saw the shape moving closer and closer.

He knew sharks could swim fast. Was it going to attack? How badly would it hurt him? He kept going, wild-eyed with terror, as Chris went crazy on the shore.

The water grew shallower. Theo was getting closer to safety . . . but not close enough yet. He felt himself overbalancing. He felt himself about to crash down into the water. He stumbled forward, put his arms out to cushion the fall and scrambled the final yard on all fours.

He had made it.

The shark had given up stalking Theo as the boy had reached the shallows. Now it was cruising around lazily in the lagoon.

Theo fell onto the sand and lay there, racked with sobs.

From clues in the story, can you tell which shark came into the lagoon?

Great White Shark: Very dangerous. Gray with white underside.

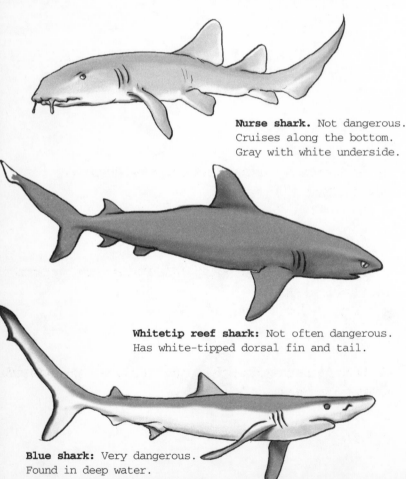

Nurse shark. Not dangerous. Cruises along the bottom. Gray with white underside.

Whitetip reef shark: Not often dangerous. Has white-tipped dorsal fin and tail.

Blue shark: Very dangerous. Found in deep water.

XTREME ADVENTURE OPERATIVE FIELD TEST 3

How would you do if you had to find your own food on a deserted island? Test your knowledge with this quiz. Keep a record of your answers and check them when you finish the story.

XTREME ADVENTURE QUIZ 3

1. Is it true or false that some seaweeds are edible?

a) True

b) False

2. Is it true or false that roasted grasshoppers are safe to eat?

a) True

b) False

3. Is it true or false that you can open a coconut with a can opener?

a) True

b) False

45

4. To harpoon a fish means to:
a) Spear it
b) Catch it in a net

5. Is it true or false that it is possible to catch some fish by tickling them?
a) True
b) False

6. Do you think it's likely that Theo's fish trap would have worked?
a) Yes
b) No

The Mask

"You're OK," Chris tried to comfort Theo, helping him up the beach to the cave entrance. They could still see the shark moving around the lagoon.

"It could have gotten me, easily," Theo sobbed.

"But it didn't," Chris attempted to reassure him. Theo's shoulders slumped, and he put his face in his hands.

"If we can't catch fish, what are we going to eat?" he wailed desperately.

"Maybe we could find some fruit or something." Chris tried to sound upbeat. "And we haven't lit a fire yet. Sitting by a fire would be good, wouldn't it? You stay here and catch your breath. I'll start piling up twigs." He didn't mention using the picture frame glass yet. He thought he'd let Theo calm down first.

"I hope they come and get us soon," he thought to himself.

He began to root around, looking for dry material to start a fire. He moved one of the stones he'd cleared from the cave, and as his hand closed over it he felt a groove. He turned it over and saw what looked like part of a carving.

"Theo, look at this," he called, as he began turning over other stones. He found four with carved marks on them. The edges of the stones had been carefully shaped, too.

"This is like some kind of jigsaw puzzle," he muttered. He positioned the four stones on the ground. They fitted together in a circle shape. The carved grooves formed an image.

Theo wandered over, and they both knelt down to study the carving.

"Are you having fun?" A harsh voice made them leap up and spin around.

A man stood pointing a gun at them. He had crept up as they peered down at the stones. He wore a wetsuit and carried a plastic sack. But what most held their horrified gaze was the disguise covering his face. It was a plastic Halloween mask with a round hole for a mouth. At a costume party it would have been funny. Here the effect was sinister and threatening.

The man walked over to the branches that Theo had tried to lash together as a raft. He kicked them apart.

"Don't bother trying to escape. The water is infested with sharks. That's why it's a good place to keep kidnap victims," he hissed.

He dropped the sack on the ground, and as he did so he noticed Theo's bag lying at the cave entrance. He flicked it open and saw the photo lying on top, where Chris had left it. He picked it up and looked at Theo.

"There you were, having a lovely time with Daddy," he sneered. "Little Theo Kitt, son of multimillionaire Errol. Such a lucky boy." He threw the photo on the ground and stamped on it viciously, cracking the glass. "Your Daddy's

going to pay big to get you back. Did you tell your little friend who you are?"

Chris was looking dumbstruck.

"Obviously not," the man chuckled viciously and then turned to Chris. "My men weren't sure which one of you was the rich boy, so they snatched you both. Still, it works out fine for me. I'll be asking Theo's kind Daddy to pay extra ransom to save you as well."

He continued in a nasty tone: "I've brought you some food, since I don't actually want you to die. Not until I get the ransom, anyway." He gestured to the sack. "My men will bring more supplies when we think you need them. So make yourselves comfortable, and pray that Daddy pays up soon."

Neither boy said anything, nor did they move. Chris was in shock. Theo looked defiant but frightened as the man turned and disappeared into the trees.

Figure out how to fit the four stones together to make a picture. What is it?

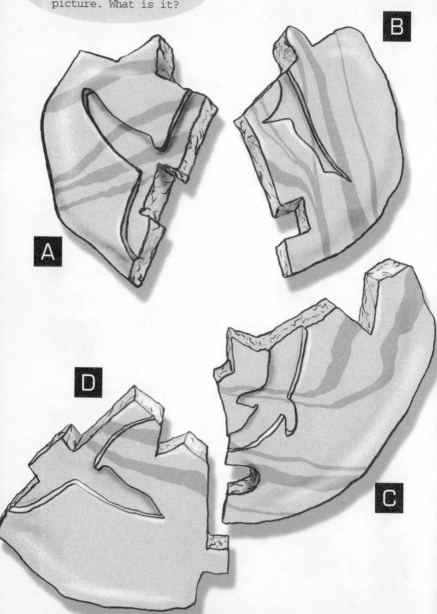

XTREME ADVENTURE QUIZ 4

1. If you had to make a bed in a cave or a shelter, would you build it from:

a) Logs

b) Stones

2. What would you put on your bed to make it more comfortable?

a) Reeds

b) Tree foliage and grass

3. If you had to build a fire, would you:

a) Pile big logs on top of small twigs?

b) Pile small twigs on top of big logs?

4. Is it true or false that all plants are edible?

a) True

b) False

5. Is it true or false that all water is safe to drink?

a) True

b) False

6. Is it true or false that you could clean your teeth with wood ash?

a) True

b) False

Trackback

Chris stared at Theo.

"You knew, didn't you?" he cried angrily. "You knew all along why we were kidnapped, because you are Errol Kitt's son and he can pay a ransom. You...you liar!"

"I never lied!" Theo cried out, but he looked guilty and awkward.

"You didn't exactly tell the truth, did you? Why?" Chris exploded.

"You hate rich people. You said so on the boat," Theo began.

"I didn't!" Chris denied it.

"You as good as said it, but that's not why I..." Theo began.

"You only thought of yourself! How selfish can you get?" Chris gasped.

"No, no, it's not like that. I didn't tell you who I was at first because of what I knew you'd think about me. But then, after we got snatched, I thought it would be too scary for you to know the truth. Wasn't it better when you didn't know? You stayed so calm and... and...practical. I just hoped Dad would get us out of here quickly."

Chris jumped up.

"I don't want anything to do with you, or your Dad!" he shouted furiously, and ran off along the beach.

Theo slumped miserably on to the sand. Things were bad enough to start with, and he'd managed to make them a lot worse. He'd been trying for hours to figure out how to tell Chris his secret. Now he'd made a mess of it, and he had to straighten things out.

Chris was so upset that he wanted to get as far away from Theo as he could. He ran in the opposite direction from the way the gunman had gone. He didn't want to see that awful mask again. He went up into the trees lining the beach. The ground gradually became steeper, leading toward the island's peak. He worked his way upward, using a stick to help him push through the foliage.

"I'm going to get to the top so I can see where to choose a new campsite, on my own," he vowed defiantly. But the slope got tougher to climb, and it took longer than he thought it would. His legs were aching when eventually the trees thinned out and left a mostly bare rocky outcrop that reflected the blazing heat of the sun.

There was a breathtaking view. The sea glittered all around the island, and Chris could make out the line of the reef stretching beyond the crescent-shaped bay.

At each corner of the bay jagged lines of rock seemed to block any possible route by foot to the opposite side of the island, where he could now see that terrifyingly steep cliffs plunged straight down into the ocean.

Chris wondered about the man in the Halloween mask. Why hadn't they seen his boat

come in through the gap in the reef? Wouldn't they have heard the engine? He didn't have to wait long to find part of the answer. He saw a motorboat emerge from under the steep side of the island and speed out to sea.

So this time the kidnapper had used a different route. But how had he gotten from the bottom of such steep cliffs all the way across to the beach?

Chris sighed. He was getting hot, frustrated, and tired, and he desperately wanted to see his mom, not struggle with so many questions.

Meanwhile, Theo had made a decision. He owed it to Chris not to sit and wait for things to happen to him, for his dad to straighten out this terrible mess. Like Chris, he had noticed that the kidnapper had not brought the motorboat through the reef. That made him determined to discover more.

The masked man had left by walking along the beach and then up into the jungle. Theo tracked his footprints in the sand, then followed the route he had taken into the trees. There was no obvious path, but Theo noticed something, a small arrow scratched on a tree. Then he saw another, and another. He guessed that they marked a route, and he followed it.

*

Chris had to get out of the sun. It was becoming unbearable up on the rock. He decided to head back down the slope, sticking to his original plan.

"I'll need to find a new campsite and maybe some fresh water," he said to himself, but as he spoke the words he already knew that his plan was impossible. There was food and water at the cave. He'd have to go back.

He sat on a rock, to rest and think about what he would say to Theo, but he was suddenly startled by a noise. Something was coming. He stood up and gripped his stick hard in case he needed to use it as a weapon.

"Chris! It's me!" Theo cried, as he emerged from the foliage. Chris dropped his stick.

"Stop creeping up on me, will you?" he snapped, but he felt relieved that it was Theo and not a wild animal or a man in a mask.

"I was looking for you," Theo replied excitedly. "I followed the kidnapper and found a route marked with arrows!"

"And?" Chris asked, fascinated.

"It led to a waterfall. Then it stopped," Theo explained. "I didn't see the masked man. I don't know where he went after that."

"I saw his boat leave from the other side of the island," Chris added to the story.

Theo reached out toward Chris. "Come back to the cave, Chris," he pleaded. "I know I was stupid, and I'm sorry. No more secrets, I promise. And I'll take you to the waterfall."

Chris nodded. He was too tired to be angry anymore.

"OK. No more secrets," he agreed. "But can we wait till tomorrow to go to the waterfall? I'm exhausted, hot, and starving. Let's go back."

That evening they sat outside the cave drinking water and eating the food the kidnapper had left. They had some cookies, sardines, and a bar of chocolate each. It wasn't a gourmet feast, but they were so hungry they didn't care.

"This island is one big, beautiful prison," Chris remarked ruefully as they watched a blazing sunset that seemed to set fire to the sea. "Does Koh's Landing look like this?" he asked.

"I don't know. I was on my way there for the first time to meet my father," Theo explained.

"Your dad's pretty famous," Chris said.

"Yeah. Sometimes it seems as if everyone in the world knows him. They read about him in the paper, I suppose. Everyone knows how rich he is," Theo said. He glanced at Chris.

"I don't tell people I meet that I'm his son because...because they start to treat me differently. They start to avoid me, or they get sort of creepy."

"I can imagine," Chris sympathized. "Listen. I'm sorry I lost it so badly before. It doesn't matter who we are, we have to work together. You must be exhausted, like me. Let's try to get some rest, then first thing tomorrow we'll hunt out the secrets of this island. Agreed?"

"Agreed," Theo nodded.

For the first time since they'd been marooned, the boys began to feel that they had gained

some control over what was happening to them.
 They knew the truth about their situation. Now
they could work to make it better.

How good would you be at tracking someone through trees? Three of these tips are correct and three are wrong. Choose the three you think will work. Keep a record of your answers and check them when you finish the story.

XTREME ADVENTURE QUIZ 5

1. Run as fast as possible.

2. Make as little noise as possible.

3. Get as close as you can to the person you are tracking.

4. Keep well back from the person you are tracking.

5. Make lots of noise to distract the person you are tracking.

6. Walk calmly.

Secrets in the Sea

With full stomachs and a long day behind them, the boys did finally get some sleep, bundling up clothes and using them as makeshift pillows. It was the kind of sleep that came and went through the night, and they frequently woke up, feeling uncomfortable and stiff.

They'd given up trying to doze any more by the time dawn broke and washed over the lagoon, turning the surface of the water gold. It looked exquisite and enticing, but now that they knew the danger lurking beneath the water, the beauty of the scene seemed like a trick.

As soon as there was enough daylight, they left the cave and followed the path that Theo had discovered. It ran from the tree line into the jungle. The way led upward, following the line of a stream through the trees until the water disappeared.

"The stream goes underground here, I think," Theo explained. "This way," he gestured.

They trudged on through the jungle, following the arrows Theo had spotted earlier, until they reached a sheer rock face rising out of the foliage. Here an arrow directed them to a narrow gap where the rock split into two from top to bottom. They squeezed into the space, shuffling sideways along the passage until it widened out again.

"Wow!" Chris gasped as they reached the other side and stepped out into a bowl of sheer rock hung with vines and vivid flower spikes. A waterfall cascaded down one side into a blue pool that filled the base of the bowl. Spray shimmered above the water in soft rainbow colors.

"It's amazing, isn't it? But I don't see any way on from here," Theo confessed. They glanced around. There were no more arrows to be seen.

They looked down at the pool. Then they looked back at each other.

"Are you a good swimmer?" Chris asked.

"Not bad," Theo replied. They kicked off their sneakers.

"Ready?" Chris said.

"Ready," Theo confirmed. They both took a step forward, grinned at each other, whooped and dived into the fresh water. Its chill sent a shock through their skin.

"Fantastic!" Chris cried as he resurfaced next to Theo. They splashed each other, laughing. Then they swam around, peering up at the sheer rock that stretched above them.

"Can you see what I see?" Theo asked, pointing. Chris stared along his finger, and realized what Theo meant. There was a symbol on the rock, partly hidden by vines. It only became clear if you looked very carefully. It appeared to be directing them behind the waterfall.

They pushed through the curtain of water. Briefly it pummeled their heads; then they came out behind it into a space between the waterfall and the rock behind it. A set of worn and slippery stairs led up toward some kind of tunnel entrance.

"The stairs look pretty old, but that's not," Theo remarked, pointing to a metal ladder that led up alongside the stairs. The boys used it to reach the tunnel opening.

"Someone's modernized the place," Chris commented, looking at a switch box hanging from a wire. He pushed a button and lit up a string of electric bulbs attached along the ceiling.

They followed the lights along the tunnel, which sloped gently downward and gradually widened until it finally opened out into a vast cavern filled with a pool. Around the edge there was a shelf of rock littered with boxes and boating equipment.

"It's some kind of base!" Theo gasped, astonished. Chris knelt down, put a finger in the water, then tasted it.

"The water here is salty," he explained and pointed to another exit leading away from the opposite side of the cavern.

"I bet that's a route to the ocean. It's big enough for a motorboat. We must be under the steep side of the island," he said.

The water in the pool was illuminated by the electric light. On the bottom they could clearly see pebbles, anemones, and some black prickly-looking sea urchins.

"I can see a little crab moving," Theo said, crouching down. "There's a tiny fish. No sharks, though," he grinned.

"Are you sure?" Chris asked, but Theo ignored him and climbed down a ladder leading to the pool surface.

"Theo!" Chris cried, but his friend was already swimming underwater. He pulled something up from beneath a rock, then resurfaced, clasping it in his hand.

"Get out, quick!" Chris insisted.

"It's OK. I don't think a shark would swim through a tunnel," Theo reassured him. "I dived in because I saw this," he explained, stroking an anemone off the small object he held in his hand. The object appeared to be made of some kind of metal. It was dulled by age, but they recognized its shape. It was in the shape of a shark.

"There's something weird about this island," Theo thought. He shuddered involuntarily, maybe because he was cold, or maybe because yet another unexplained mystery had appeared, as if from nowhere.

How much do you think you know about sharks? Try this quiz, keep a record of your answers, and find out if you were right after you finish the story.

XTREME ADVENTURE QUIZ 6

1. Are sharks:
a) A type of fish?
b) A type of mammal?

2. Which of these answers is true?
a) Sharks live only in warm waters.
b) Some sharks like warm waters and some prefer cold waters.

3. Which of these answers is true?
a) All sharks will attack people.
b) Only some sharks will attack people.

75

4. Which one of these is a type of shark?

a) Bluetooth

b) Hammerhead

5. The world's biggest shark is the whale shark. It can grow up to:

a) 13 feet (4m) long

b) 45 feet (14m) long

6. Which one of these is a type of shark?

a) Sand tiger

b) Red eye

A Mystery in a Mystery

The boys scrabbled around the rim of the cavern, poking about in the hoard of equipment the kidnappers had left behind.

"I guess they never thought we'd find our way here," Theo remarked. Chris took a look inside a couple of boxes. One of them contained newspaper clippings.

"Look at this, Theo!" He turned around and immediately jumped back with a gasp. "Don't DO that to me!" he cried. Theo was standing right next to him wearing the Halloween mask they had seen worn by the leader of the kidnap gang.

"Sorry, I just found it on top of a box." Theo

took it off and smiled. "It proves that the man came back this way yesterday."

"And these reports are proof his gang has been running a kidnapping operation for a while," Chris replied, handing Theo a bundle of clippings. Theo read out some headlines:

"Property Heiress Alicia Brown Disappears on Vacation"

"Heiress Returned After Family Pays Large Ransom"

There were two or three other similar stories. Victims were kidnapped, then returned after payment. In each case they had refused to say where they had been kept, because they had been threatened with violent reprisals.

"It has to be the same gang. Why else would they keep these reports? Do you think they've held their kidnap victims on this island before?" Theo wondered.

"I don't know. Maybe . . . " Chris replied. "Come

to think of it, do you remember when we first went into the trees to try to make a shelter? I think I saw the letters AB scratched on a tree. That could have been Alicia Brown, leaving her mark."

An unhappy look crossed Theo's face for the first time in a while. "My dad told me that rich people get kidnapped for money more and more these days. He wanted me to have a bodyguard on this trip, and we had an argument about it. I said I didn't want to be followed everywhere. He said I was being difficult. I guess I was," he sighed glumly.

Chris thought to himself how glad he was to have led an ordinary life. Well, it *had* been ordinary. He was in Theo's world now, and that was anything *but* normal.

"I won't let the kidnappers win this time," Theo insisted fiercely.

"I'm with you all the way," Chris agreed. "Let's keep scouting around. We might find some more useful stuff."

Besides the wide channel that led to the ocean, there were three smaller cave entrances off the main cavern. Theo climbed down into the pool and swam over to inspect them. Two proved to be dead ends. One was partly filled with water but seemed to lead around a corner into darkness. Theo swam into it and disappeared from view. Chris could hear him splashing; then the noise stopped.

"Theo, are you OK?" Chris asked anxiously.

"Yes, it's fine. Follow me!" Theo cried. Chris glanced around nervously. Would a shark come this far in from the sea? Theo was right. Probably not. Still, he had to force himself to enter the water and swim through the tunnel.

There was enough reflection from the cavern's light for him to see that Theo had climbed out and was sitting on a ledge. Chris pulled himself up alongside Theo.

The ledge receded back into the rock. In the cavity, just visible, there was another box, but this one looked much older than the storage boxes in the main cavern. It was made partly of intricately decorated metal.

"It's covered with sharks," Chris observed, running his hand over the writhing shapes, tracing them with his finger.

Between them they managed to drag the box forward. It was very heavy, and there was no obvious way to open it. There were no lid clasps or locks.

Theo felt in his pocket and pulled out the flat metal sharkshape he had found at the bottom of the pool.

"At last I think we may be able to solve one of the mysteries we've found," he murmured, and tried to fit it into one of the sharkshapes on the box surface. It didn't quite match. He tried another, then another. The third time it fitted perfectly. He pushed hard, and there was a loud clicking sound as the box lid sprang open.

Inside there was a carefully folded piece of cloth. It was obviously old but still in fairly good condition. The boys carefully lifted it. Its color was faded now but had probably once been a vivid silken red. A black shark emblem stretched across the center.

"It looks like some kind of flag," Chris suggested.

"Wow! Check these out!" Theo added, pointing

at two beautifully engraved guns nestling in some old coins.

"It's a pair of old pistols," he announced excitedly. "Do you think they could be made of silver? And who could have left them here?"

"We've found yet another mystery to add to the list." Chris shook his head in amazement.

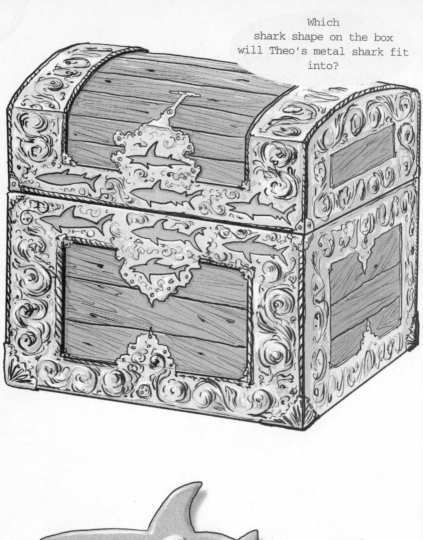

How much do you know about pirates?
Three of the answers below are
correct and the rest are false.
Choose the three you think are
right. Keep a record of your
answers and check them when
you finish the story.

XTREME ADVENTURE QUIZ 7

1. A group of pirate ships together would be called a squadron.

2. Some famous pirates were women.

3. Pirates from Southeast Asia sailed boats called sloopers.

4. A group of pirate ships together would be called a fleet.

5. Blackbeard was a famous pirate-catcher.

6. Pirates from Southeast Asia sailed boats called junks.

A Trap is Set

"If we knew the kidnappers were coming we could be ready for them and maybe set a trap," Chris thought, as they made their way back into the cavern, carefully carrying their new-found treasures above the water.

Theo climbed out and made his way around to the exit leading to the sea. He pointed to some marks painted on the wall.

"These marks look as if they show the level of the water at high and low tide and each hour in between. The sea must rise in the cavern and in the tunnel entrance, too. It wouldn't be a problem in the cavern, but in the tunnel there wouldn't be enough space between the water and the roof of the tunnel for a boat to come through at high tide," Theo explained.

"And the tides change..." Chris began.

"... every six hours," Theo finished his sentence for him. "OK, let's work this out. Say the tide starts going out. I figure it would take maybe two hours for the water level to go down enough for a boat to get through here. Then for eight hours the water would be low enough for the boat to come in and out."

"So if we can calculate the tide times, we'll know roughly when to keep watch for the boat on the horizon," Chris added. "You're a genius, Theo!"

"I do my best," Theo grinned. "I really like sailing, so I know a little about the tides."

"Do you think they'd bring the boat in at night?" Chris asked.

"I'd guess not. It would be too dangerous near the cliffs and rocks," Theo replied. "And I don't think they'd bring it in as the water started to rise up from the low-tide point. They'd risk getting stuck on the island for too long. So we're talking about a period of four hours, starting from two hours after high tide, during daylight, when they're likely to arrive."

"And we'll be ready," Chris declared.

They sat on the boxes and made their escape plans there and then. Afterward they returned the way they had come, through the pool and along the arrowed path back to the beach.

When they reached the cave, they kept an eye on the level of the lagoon and the ferocity of the waves clattering up against the reef. When the level rose to its highest, and the waves were at their largest, they knew the tide was in. They kept a note of the exact time.

The next day, when they knew the tide was going out, they climbed the hill in the center of the island and sat under the shade of a tree but with a good view of the horizon.

They repeated the pattern for two more days, with no sighting of a boat. But they were sure they'd have a visit soon because their food and water supplies were running low. Finally, on the fourth day of watching and waiting, Chris cried: "There's the boat! Come on!" he urged.

They rushed down the hill and along the path to the pool and the waterfall. Once they were inside the cavern, they hid behind the boxes.

The roar of a boat engine echoed around the walls as the motorboat came into view, edging its way through the tunnel from the sea. Both boys felt a surge of fear. Even though they'd planned for this moment, it was hard to stay calm and not run away.

There was one man in the boat. It was clear that he wasn't the gang leader; he was shorter and a different shape. They recognized him as one of the gunmen who had first snatched them. He moored the boat, shouldered a plastic sack full of food supplies, and stepped out of the boat.

He looked around. Had he heard the boys breathing, or maybe seen their shadows? He walked toward their hiding place and reached over. Then his hand stopped and picked up the Halloween mask that lay on the box where Theo had left it.

Both boys unconsciously held their breath until, to their huge relief, the man turned away from them. He took the mask and went off through the exit that led to the waterfall. The boys nodded to each other.

"Plan A," Theo whispered.

They stepped out from behind the boxes and moved toward the boat.

"Hey!" the man's voice shouted behind them. For some reason he'd turned back. He roared angrily and ran toward them.

"Plan B!" Theo shouted. The boys had decided what they would do if something went wrong. Now they had to use that emergency back-up plan, and fast.

Theo grabbed the old silver pistols he'd positioned within easy reach, and though he knew they weren't loaded, he brandished them as if they were.

The man faltered when he saw that Theo had weapons in his hand. His split-second hesitation allowed Chris to make a move.

As the man reached for his own gun, Chris hurled a box at him. It hit him right in the chest and he lost his balance. His face registered surprise as he fell backward. Another box thudded into his side, and he toppled into the water.

The boys leaped on to the motorboat, and Chris slipped the mooring line off its post. He had to work rapidly. The man had resurfaced and was swimming toward them.

Theo had piloted a boat before, but a much smaller one. This version was more powerful, but luckily it had roughly the same controls. He looked them over. The key was in the ignition. There was a red start button and a throttle lever.

"Quick!" Chris cried, as the man grabbed at the side of the boat.

For a moment Theo's mind went blank with panic. Then the information he needed flashed back into his brain, and he pushed the red button.

The engine roared into life, and the boat lurched forward. Theo spun it around. Its rubber edges bumped clumsily on the cavern wall. He felt Chris topple down into the back of the boat. He couldn't see the man in the water. Then a shout alerted him.

The man had climbed out and was pointing his gun at them. Theo aimed for the seaward exit

and ducked down just as a shot rang out. It ricocheted off the wall as they entered the tunnel.

"Slow down!" Chris screamed as the boat crashed from one wall to the other. Theo grabbed the throttle and slowed the boat down. They'd turned a corner, and the man wouldn't be able to shoot at them now, though they could still hear him shouting furiously in the background.

Worryingly, the tunnel narrowed instead of widening, and they scraped the sides more than once. When the ocean finally came into sight they saw that the tunnel exit was very small. A swell of water was funneling into it, pitching up and down.

Theo had to get the timing right and reach the exit exactly as the water troughed. If it rose underneath them at the wrong moment it might pin them up against the ceiling, and then possibly even flip the boat as it plunged back down.

Theo slowed the speed. He had to pick just the right moment. The swell rose and pushed them dangerously upward. Then it fell again, and he opened the throttle.

The boat sped out the entrance, and they both whooped. Then Theo steered out toward the open sea. At first he went too fast, and the boat reared up. The engine screamed as the prop came out of the water.

"Theo!"Chris hollered.

"OK, OK, I've got it," Theo reassured him and slowed the speed. He felt in a pocket and took out the map of islands that he had first brought with him.

"Let's head for Koh's Landing," he cried.

XTREME ADVENTURE OPERATIVE FIELD TEST 8

XTREME ADVENTURE QUIZ 8

1. What causes the tides?
a) The pull of the moon
b) The pull of the stars

2. How many oceans are there in the world?
a) 8
b) 5

3. Is it true or false that seawater is salty only when the tide is high?
a) True
b) False

4. Is it true or false that every type of fish can live in the sea?

a) True

b) False

5. What is a sea urchin?

a) A type of sea plant

b) A type of sea animal

6. What do people call a big hurricane storm in Southeast Asia?

a) A pontoon

b) A typhoon

Through the Sharks

They saw the sharks after twenty minutes or so when they slowed down to get their bearings. Two fins, alarmingly large, circled the boat methodically, first at a distance and then in closer.

"I like being close to nature, but this is freaking me out," Theo admitted.

"Maybe they're just curious," Chris replied nervously, but every time he glanced at them his stomach clenched with fear.

This phase of their escape had seemed easy when they'd discussed stealing the boat. Now it was proving tougher than they'd imagined. They'd planned for the sun beating down on them as they crossed the water, and they were wearing hats, but the intense heat quickly tired them.

Though they had their island map, they didn't know anything about the ocean currents of the area, and that was a big worry. They just had to hope their luck would last, the wind would stay light, and the boat would hold out.

They passed a couple of small, uninhabited islands. Then they saw a boat in the distance. It looked like a harmless fishing boat, but they decided not to take the chance of making contact.

"We don't know who our friends are. The man we left behind might have had a radio and alerted the rest of the gang to catch us," Theo suggested anxiously.

After what seemed like ages, Chris pointed toward the horizon.

"Koh's Landing should be coming into view soon," he said hopefully.

They scanned the seascape. It seemed to go on forever. Had they gotten it all wrong and put themselves into a worse situation than before, abandoned in a shark-infested sea?

"There!" Chris cried. A low, dark mound appeared on the very edge of the horizon line.

"Land ahoy!" Theo shouted. "And look...the sharks are gone."

"Maybe they were just escorting us home," Chris grinned.

As they rounded the island a small harbor came into view, below a group of attractive new buildings. A few people were at the water's edge. As the boys motored toward the harbor nobody paid much attention to them at first. People craned to look only when Chris started waving and yelling excitedly.

"Mom! Mom! It's me!"

A woman jumped up from her seat by the harbor wall and ran toward the beach. When the boys finally leaped out of the boat she was waiting to envelop Chris in a hug.

"Chris, thank goodness you're safe," she exclaimed, and then broke down in tears. Other people were shouting now, and soon a tall man ran down from the buildings beyond.

"Theo!" he bellowed.

"Dad, I'm OK..." Theo began, but his voice was muffled by his dad's big bear hug.

The boys were taken to Errol Kitt's office, where they were given food and water. They explained how they'd been dumped on an uninhabited island, how they'd found the kidnappers' secret base and then escaped.

When they had finished, Theo's dad looked solemn and troubled.

"I've been trying to arrange for the money to pay the gang. When I was contacted for a ransom I was told not to involve the police, or you'd be harmed. Thank heavens you're safe," he declared. He gave them a strange look. "Did you say the gang leader wore a Halloween mask?" he asked quietly.

"Yes, to hide his face," Theo confirmed. "It was creepy, with a big hole for a mouth."

Theo's dad reached up and took a framed photograph off his office wall. He handed it to the boys. Theo gasped and Chris pointed.

"There's the mask! It's exactly the same," he insisted.

The photo showed a group of people dressed

for a party. One of them wore the distinctive mask with an "o" for a mouth.

"That photo was taken on the night of our opening party here," Theo's dad explained. "The person you are pointing to is my chief hotel manager, John Thackery. I can't believe he has anything to do with a gang. There's no way he would get involved in this."

There was a commotion outside. Chris turned and peered out the window toward the harbor. "Someone's taking the boat," he cried. They watched as a man boarded the motorboat and maneuvered it away from its mooring, at the same time pointing a gun at frightened onlookers on the shore.

"That's John Thackery," Theo's dad exclaimed, outraged. At that moment the man aimed his gun toward their window.

"Get down!" Theo shouted as a bullet slammed into the wall outside. Then more smashed into the window.

"He'll escape!" Theo cried.

"Let him," his dad replied.

"But the gang...you can't let them get away,"

Theo gasped.

"You two boys have behaved fantastically. Theo, I have never felt so proud in my life. And Chris, too. I'm grateful for your help. I'm not going to let you down. John Thackery and his men will be caught, and I know just who to contact to make that happen."

Theo's dad made a phone call to Xtreme Adventure Headquarters.

"I should have done this earlier," he muttered. "I've called in the experts. Special agents will be arriving tomorrow. You'll need to tell them all you know. In the meantime, get cleaned up, rest, and don't worry. Xtreme Adventure doesn't let people down either."

As they got up to leave something outside one of the office windows caught Chris's eye.

"What's that?" he asked, gesturing toward a flag that flew outside. It had a red background with a black shark across its center, just like the one they'd found back in the cavern on the island. Theo saw it and shook his head in disbelief. It seemed that things weren't straightforward yet. There was at least one more mystery for them to handle.

"That's a copy of the flag that the legendary pirate Koh used, the pirate we named the resort after. The shark was his symbol," Theo's dad explained.

"Legend has it Koh ran a secret island base around here, though nobody has ever found it. The story goes that he had a young son whom he loved dearly. One day this boy fell into the sea, but the sharks miraculously did not attack him. After that the shark became Koh's talisman, his good-luck symbol."

Chris and Theo glanced at each other.

"I think we know where that base is, Dad," Theo replied. He explained about the carved stones they'd found, the symbol by the waterfall, and the old pistols and flag they'd discovered hidden in the shark-covered box of coins. Sadly they'd left the pistols stowed on the floor in the motorboat. John Thackery had them now, but this was a small loss compared to the safety they had gained.

The only thing Theo left out of his account of their time on the island was the incident when he'd been in the lagoon with the shark. He'd agreed with Chris that they'd keep it quiet, so as not to scare their parents too much. Now he wondered if the shark had deliberately spared him, like the boy in the legend. They would never know for sure, but that private shared mystery was the reason Chris and Theo both wore shark symbols as good-luck charms from that day on!

A good XTREME ADVENTURE operative must have a sharp memory. Find out how much you remember from the story you have just read. Keep a record of your answers and check them in the final section of the book.

XTREME ADVENTURE QUIZ 9

1. What was Theo's dad's full name?

2. What happened to the first shelter that Chris and Theo built?

3. What did Chris find in Theo's bag?

109

4. What did the boys find inside the box decorated with sharks?

5. What was the name of the leader of the kidnap gang?

6. How did the boys find out the true identity of the leader of the kidnap gang?

XTREME ADVENTURE INC.

SHARK ISLAND MYSTERY
MISSION REPORT

TOP SECRET

AUTHORIZED AGENTS ONLY

MISSION REPORT:

Errol Kitt, Theo's dad, contacted XTREME ADVENTURE INC. as soon as he discovered that the boys were safe. He knew of our expertise in dealing with criminal gangs.

There was a powerful case against John Thackery, the gang leader. We had to find him and stop him from continuing his crimes.

A message from

XTREME ADVENTURE INC.

Situation judged **URGENT.**

Action taken:

Theo and Chris had enough detailed evidence for us to pinpoint the kidnappers' island base. Our agents landed on the island immediately.

Result:

One of the kidnappers had been left on the island when the boys stole his boat. He was caught and disarmed. He gave evidence that identified the other gang members.

Follow-up work:

The rest of the gang was rounded up and handed to police. The leader, John Thackery, disappeared but gave himself away when he later tried to sell the silver pistols he'd found in the motorboat. We were ready and waiting to catch him red-handed.

AGENT REPORT: CHRIS BROWN

Chris Brown was recommended as ideal future material for XTREME ADVENTURE INC. training. He showed practicality, sensitivity to others, and bravery. He was quick-thinking and was able to work well in a team.

Mistakes made: Chris chose a bad position to build the first shelter. At one point he also argued with Theo when they should have tried to work together at all times.

Recommendation: During training, concentrate on survival skills.

Update: Following training, Chris Brown became a top operative.

Location: Worldwide

Code name: Quarterback

Alias: Tourist, football fan, or friend of Operative Alias "Sailor"

AGENT REPORT: THEO KITT

Theo Kitt was recommended as ideal future material for XTREME ADVENTURE INC. training. He showed good thinking skills, tracking skills, and practical sailing skills. He was brave and ready to undertake challenges, and he was also prepared to admit his mistakes and learn from them.

Mistakes made: He did not tell Chris his true identity from the beginning, so at first they did not work as a team. Did not have survival skills.

Recommendation: During training, concentrate on survival skills such as building shelters.

Update: Following training, Theo Kitt became an excellent operative.

Location: Worldwide

Code name: Sailor

Alias: Rich yacht-owner

SPECIAL EXTRA REPORT

Shark Island proved to be a very interesting historical site and contained many relics from centuries of pirate occupation.

The two fine silver pistols dating from the time of the infamous pirate Koh were auctioned for a large sum. The money was used to preserve the island as a nature sanctuary.

YOUR AGENT REPORT

Did you pass the tests as well as Chris and Theo? Score your answers to the puzzles and quizzes. Then take the ultimate **ELITE SQUAD** island test on page 125.

Operative Field Test 1

Score 2 for the correct answer.

This is the island. It is the only one with a crescent-shaped bay, beach, reef, and hill rising up from the middle.

Quiz 1 Score 1 for each correct answer.

1. a) A bank of rocky material. **2.** b) A stretch of shallow seawater. **3.** a) Jungle **4.** a) Very calm **5.** a) The outside edge of the reef, facing the ocean. **6.** b) Southeast Asia

Operative Field Test 2

Score 1 for each correct answer.

There is an empty drink can. There is a flip-flop, a rope, and the carved initials AB on a tree.

Quiz 2 Score 1 for each correct answer.
1. a) It might flood. **2.** b) Downwind, so smells get blown away from your tent. **3.** b) Level ground. On sloping ground you might roll out.

4. b) Recently dropped branches. Dead, dry branches would snap more easily.

5. a) Leaf-covered branches. Mud would be too heavy and would wash away.

6. a) Facing away from the wind, to give you better shelter.

Operative Field Test 3

Score 4 for the correct answer: It was a whitetip reef shark. It was not aggressive, and it had white tips on its dorsal fin.

Quiz 3 Score 1 for each correct answer.
1. a) True. Some seaweeds are edible after cooking, though not all seaweeds. **2.** a) True
3. b) False. It is very hard to open a coconut.
4. a) Spear it **5.** a) True **6.** b) Most likely not. A fish wouldn't find its way through a small bottleneck.

Operative Field Test 4

Score 2 for the correct answer:
The picture shows a shark. This is how the stones fit together.

A C D B

Quiz 4 Score 1 for each correct answer.

1. a) Logs. Stones are colder and harder. **2.** b) Tree foliage and grass would be softest and easiest to collect. **3.** a) Pile big logs on top of small twigs. The twigs will help get the fire going. **4.** b) False. Many plants are poisonous. Don't try experimenting! **5.** b) Lots of water is unsafe, for example, stagnant water or water from a polluted stream. **6.** a) True

Operative Field Test 5

Score 1 for each arrow you spotted.

Quiz 5 Score 1 for each correct answer.

The correct tips are: **2.** Make as little noise as possible. **4.** Keep far back from the person you are tracking, so they don't see you. **6.** Walk calmly so as not to alert the person, make too much noise, or trip.

Operative Field Test 6

Score 2 for the correct answer:
There is a shark shape on the rock. Its nose points toward the waterfall.

Quiz 6 Score 1 for each correct answer.

1. a) Sharks are a type of fish. **2.** b) Some sharks like warm waters; some prefer cold waters. **3.** b) Only some sharks will attack people. **4.** b) Hammerhead **5.** b) Whale sharks can grow to 45 feet long. They are harmless to humans. **6.** a) Sand tiger

Operative Field Test 7

Score 3 for the correct answer:

Quiz 7 Score 1 for each correct answer.
The three correct answers are:

2. Some famous pirates were women, including Southeast Asian pirate leaders.

4. A group of pirate ships together would be called a fleet.

7. Pirates from Southeast Asia sailed boats called junks.

Modern pirates use machine guns and speedboats instead of pistols, swords or junks. Blackbeard was a famous pirate, not a pirate-catcher.

Operative Field Test 8

Score 4 for the correct answer.
The tides change every six hours, so if low tide is at 8 A.M., high tide will be at 2 P.M., six hours later. The boys calculate it is safe for a boat to enter the tunnel two hours after high tide, which would be 4 P.M.

Quiz 8 Score 1 for each correct answer.
1. a) The pull of the moon. **2.** b) Five (Arctic, Atlantic, Pacific, Southern, Indian) **3.** b) False. The sea is always salty. **4.** b) False. Freshwater fish cannot normally live in salty water. They live only in fresh water such as rivers or lakes. **5.** b) A type of animal. **6.** b) A typhoon.

Operative Field Test 9

Score 1 for each shark. There are six.

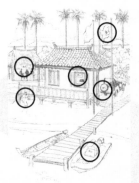

Quiz 9 Score 1 for each correct answer.
1. Errol Kitt **2.** It was blown down by a storm. **3.** A photograph in a frame. **4.** An old flag and two pistols. **5.** John Thackery **6.** They saw a photo of him wearing the Halloween mask.

Total up your score out of a possible 80

Score of 1–30

You need to brush up on your skills. Better luck next time.

Score of 31–51

You almost made it! Try another XTREME ADVENTURE to make the grade.

Score 52–80

Good job! You have passed! You're good enough to be an XTREME ADVENTURE operative.

PASS CONFIRMED

FILE No. 1336-8 XA

Welcome to:
XTREME ADVENTURE INC

Now you are ready to take:

THE ELITE SQUAD ISLAND
TEST

Kidnap victims have been on the island before. One of them, Alicia Brown, scratched her initials, **AB**, all around the island. You know there is one on page 30, but where are the other four? Find them all to join our ELITE SQUAD, used for top missions.

On a trip with his parents to the Amazon, Simon suddenly finds himself alone in the depths of the rain forest. How will he communicate with the local people? What dangers lie in wait for him? And will he be able to rescue his parents from the evil gang that hold them captive? Join in the action and figure out your own survival skills in the next exciting XTREME ADVENTURE INC.

title:
Attack of the Jaguar

XTREME ADVENTURE INC

THE SCORPION SECRET

DARE TO TAKE THE TEST

COULD YOU SURVIVE IN THE BAKING EGYPTIAN DESERT?

A holiday in Egypt suddenly becomes dangerous for Tom and his big stepbrother, Zak. What is the secret of the Scorpion? Who abandoned them in the desert? What exactly is hiding inside the Scorpion Tomb? Join in the action and figure out your own survival skills in the next exciting XTREME ADVENTURE INC.

title:
The Scorpion Secret

A long-awaited fishing trip with his grandfather becomes a nightmare for Joe when he gets lost in the Canadian bear forest. Can he escape a bear attack? Why is the lake surrounded by dead animals? Will the legendary Spirit Bear guide him home? Join in the action and figure out your own survival skills in the next exciting XTREME ADVENTURE INC.

title:
The Riddle of Bear Cave